James Edward Homans

Our Three Admirals - Farragut, Porter, Dewey

An authentic account of the heroic characters, distinguished careers, and

memorable achievements of the three officers, who have attained the

highest rank in the navy of the United States

James Edward Homans

Our Three Admirals - Farragut, Porter, Dewey
An authentic account of the heroic characters, distinguished careers, and
memorable achievements of the three officers, who have attained the highest rank
in the navy of the United States

ISBN/EAN: 9783337196028

Printed in Europe, USA, Canada, Australia, Japan

Cover: Foto ©Raphael Reischuk / pixelio.de

More available books at **www.hansebooks.com**

OUR
THREE ADMIRALS

FARRAGUT   PORTER
DEWEY

AN AUTHENTIC ACCOUNT OF THE HEROIC
CHARACTERS, DISTINGUISHED CAREERS, AND
MEMORABLE ACHIEVEMENTS OF THE THREE
OFFICERS WHO HAVE ATTAINED THE HIGHEST
RANK IN THE NAVY OF THE UNITED STATES

WITH PORTRAITS, MAPS, AND ILLUSTRATIONS

BY

JAMES E. HOMANS

Editorial Staff of the National Cyclopædia of
American Biography

Exigui numero, sed bello vivida virtus.—VIRGIL

NEW YORK
JAMES T. WHITE & CO.
1899

CONTENTS.

PREFACE.

In these days when the naval supremacy of the United States seems about to be regained, as a result of the unparalleled record of the late war with Spain, and in the new fleet of powerful fighting ships almost ready for commission, it seems timely to propose a brief study of the careers of the three officers who have held the highest rank and title in the service. It is interesting to note what we might almost call the close succession in the highest honors. Both Porter and Farragut were trained for their heroic careers by that old fighter of 1812-15, Captain David Porter, who achieved a glorious defeat with his ship "Essex," lowering his flag only when his strength was spent. These two foster-brothers achieved fame together in the Mississippi, where Dewey's genius also awoke to deeds of daring. Both of them held rank as Commander—Dewey, as Lieutenant—but, as in a day, they sprang into an undying renown.

Although dogged courage is a quality for which the American Navy has ever been noted, it is in the manner of its expression that we may trace the influence of a supreme master. Schley learned of Farragut that every danger must be dared in the pursuit of duty, and it was this grand lesson grandly learned that brought him safely through the Arctic ice-pack, that had thwarted two previous expeditions, and won him fame as the rescuer of Greely. Captain Gridley was mindful of Farragut's stern discipline, when, ill to death as he was, he insisted on fighting his ship at Manila. "Going to Manila killed me," he said, "but I would do it again if

v

necessary." Captain Sigsbee. stepping from the wreck of the "Maine," to send his famous cablegram "Suspend judgment," showed himself another hero of the Farragut mould.

Besides these three, we might mention among the disciples of the Admirals, Captain Charles E. Clark, who was ensign on the "Ossipee" in Mobile Bay ; Captain Francis A. Cook, who was ensign on the "Genesee" ; Rear-Admiral John C. Watson, who was lieutenant on the " Hartford," and Rear-Admiral Montgomery Sicard. who was lieutenant on the "Oneida." Captains Henry C. Taylor and Robley D. Evans were both ensigns in the North Atlantic Squadron, under Admiral Porter, and participated in his famous assault on and capture of Fort Fisher.

The biographies included in this book were enlarged from those prepared originally for the " National Cyclopædia of American Biography." They were carefully compiled from the best accessible authorities, and in order to insure the utmost accuracy, were referred in each case to the judgment of close relatives of the subjects, as is the invariable rule in the preparation of sketches for this cyclopædia. Thus the sketch of Farragut was submitted to his son, Loyall Farragut, of New York City; that of Porter to his son, R. B. Porter, U.S.N.; and that of Dewey to his son, George G. Dewey, of New York City, later to his sister, resident in Montpelier, Vt , and finally to the Admiral himself. Their accuracy is thus assured.

LIST OF ILLUSTRATIONS.

..

DAVID G. FARRAGUT

OUR THREE ADMIRALS

FARRAGUT

D AVID GLASGOW FARRAGUT, the first Admiral of the United States Navy, was born at **BIRTH AND PARENTAGE** Campbell's Station, near Knoxville, Tenn., July 5, 1801, son of George and Elizabeth (Shine) Farragut.

His father (1755–1817), a native of Ciudadela, Island of Minorca, came to America in 1776, and, like Kosciusko, Steuben, Pulaski, and other Europeans, espoused the American **FATHER'S CAREER** cause. He served in the cavalry of the Continental Army, and participated in many engagements, notably the Battle of Cowpens, where he is said to have saved the life of General Washington. After the war he resided at various places in Tennessee and

Louisiana, and was Muster-Master for the District
of Washington (Eastern Tennessee), with the rank
of Major (1792–93). Early in the Nineteenth
Century he entered the Naval Service; served in
1810 as Sailing-Master of the expedition dispatched by Governor William C. C. Claiborne, of
Louisiana, to take possession of the disputed
territory on the Gulf coast of Mississippi and
Louisiana; was for a time Magistrate of Pasca-
goula County, and accompanied his friend,
General Jackson, on his Indian campaigns in
1813–14. He was married some years after the
Revolution to a daughter of John and Ellenor
(McIven) Shine, of Dobbs County, N. C., who
bore him three sons and two daughters.

The family, known variously as Farragut or
Ferragut, was an old one in the Balearic Islands;
THE FAMILY the line being traceable through
numerous distinguished person-
ages to the Thirteenth Century, when Don
Pedro Ferragut won fame and property under
King Iago I., of Aragon, surnamed *El Con-
quistador*, in the campaigns against the Moors.
During the Fifteenth and Sixteenth Cen-
turies thirteen representatives of the family

are recorded councilors of the kingdom of
Majorca; three were magistrates of the City of
Palma; one, Augustin Ferragut, a noted theo-
logian, was Prebendary of the Cathedral of Palma
and Benefactor of the House of Repentants there;
another, Pablo Ferragut, was Topographer and
Historian of Majorca, and another, Captain
Antonio Ferragut, won distinction under Philip
IV. of Spain, and bequeathed his property to
found a college, which is still in existence. The
Admiral's grandfather, Antonio Ferragut, son of
Jorge and Ursula (Guitart) Fer-   **GRAND-**
ragut, was married to Juana   **PARENTS**
Mesquida, of Ciudadela, whose surname seems
to have supplanted that of her husband in the
Island of Minorca. In other parts of Spain,
however, representatives of the family are still
found in prominent official and ecclesiastical
positions; Gonzolo Ferragut, a native of Pollenza,
and a member of the Dominican Order, was made
Bishop of Urgel in 1827, and of Yoiza in 1831,
where he continued until his death, in 1843;
during the Spanish-American War of 1898 there
was an officer in the Spanish naval service bearing the same family name.

David G. Farragut, the most illustrious of this long and notable line, never knew childhood in the ordinary sense, his early

CHILDHOOD

years being filled with wild adventures in the Indian country, and the almost equally hazardous exploits of his father, who appears to have been afraid of nothing on sea or land. When scarcely eight years of age, he lost his mother by yellow fever, her death occurring in the same house and at the same time with that of David Porter, Sailing-Master in the United States Navy, at New Orleans, and father of Commodore David Porter, who succeeded to the office, and shortly afterward adopted young Farragut into his family. This was the real beginning of his naval career; for, after a little over a year's schooling in Washington, D. C., and Chester, Pa., he received an appointment as midshipman in the Navy, December 10, 1810.

He made his first voyage under Captain Porter on the frigate "Essex," of 32 guns, and spent the next two years, until the

FIRST SERVICE

outbreak of the War of 1812, in alternate cruising and schooling. When war was declared, the " Essex " was attached to a small squadron brought together in New York harbor, consisting, beside herself, of the " President " and the " Hornet." Putting to sea at once, the " Essex " opened hostilities by capturing several

ACTION BETWEEN THE "ESSEX" AND "ALERT."

British vessels, notably the " Alert " of 20 guns, which she took after a fight of seven minutes. Later, while lying in the Delaware River, Captain Porter received orders to join Commodore Bainbridge's squadron in West Indian waters, and cruise with him in the track of British merchantmen, or, failing to overtake him, to act at his own discretion. The result was the memorable voyage of the " Essex " in the Pacific Ocean,

in the course of which she touched at several
islands of the Marquesas and Galapagos groups,
VOYAGE IN and captured numerous prizes.
THE PACIFIC Farragut's account of this
voyage in his journal abounds in interesting
episodes of adventure and prowess, such as
characterized the naval service of that day.
Finally, having run into the harbor of Valparaiso,
in January, 1814, the " Essex " was met by the
British frigates " Phœbe " and " Cherub," which
kept her blockaded for over six weeks. On
March 28th she attempted to escape, and would
probably have succeeded had not her mainmast
gone by the board, and caused Captain Porter to
attempt to return into the harbor.* This proved
a fatal mistake, and, if we may judge from Farragut's statement, was a wholly unnecessary
move. He says : " I consider our original and
greatest mistake was in attempting to regain the
anchorage ; as, being greatly superior to the
enemy in sailing qualities, I think we should have
borne up and run before the wind. . . . Then
we could   .   have passed on, leaving both

---

* See chapter on David D. Porter for further account of this
incident.

vessels behind, until we had replaced our top-mast, by which time they would have been separated, as, unless they did so, it would have been no chase, the 'Cherub' being a dull sailer.''

As it was, Porter found himself at the mercy of both British vessels, and after a fight seldom exceeded for gallantry and perseverance, in course of which his ship was nearly destroyed, he was obliged to surrender. Although little more than thirteen years of age, Farragut bore a distinguished part in this action, being, to use his own words, "a man on occasions," performing the duties of quarter-gunner, powder-boy, and, in fact, everything that was required. In his

BATTLE WITH THE "PHOEBE" AND "CHERUB"

official report, Captain Porter specially recommended him for bravery; expressing regret that he was " too young to be eligible for promotion." After the action he volunteered as surgeon's assistant, and, as he says, "never earned Uncle Sam's money so faithfully " as then, rising at daybreak to arrange bandages and plasters, and spending most of the day attending the patients in various ways.

Shortly after his return to New York he was again put to school at Chester, Pa., this time under a "queer old individual named Neif," one of Napoleon's famous Old Guard, who had the

ON THE GUN DECK OF THE "ESSEX."

original method of teaching orally, and without books, requiring the pupils to take notes and pass examinations. In November, 1814, he was ordered to the brig "Spark," one of the squadron fitted out under Commodore Porter to prey on the enemy's commerce. Peace had been declared, however, before the fleet was ready for sea, so his commission was changed to the frigate "Indepen-

LATER
SEA-SERVICE

dence," as aide to Captain William M. Crane. The "Independence" sailed for the Barbary coast, but arrived too late to take part in the CRUISE ON THE "INDE- PENDENCE" Algerine War, and after cruising through the Mediterranean Sea, returned home.

After passing the winter in Boston harbor, Farragut was transferred to the "Macedonian," and later to the "Washington," Captain Creighton, flagship of Commodore Chauncey. "The captain," writes Farragut, "was the greatest martinet in the service. We had what is called a 'crack ship'; that is, she was in beautiful order, with the greatest qua tity of 'bright work,' clean decks, and a well-drilled crew for performing their duty with dispatch. But all this was CRUISE ON THE "WASH- INGTON" accomplished at the sacrifice of the comfort of every one on board. My experience in the matter, instead of making me a proselyte to the doctrine of the old officers on this subject, determined me never to have a 'crack ship,' if it was only to be attained by such means." In this ship he made a voyage over the Mediterranean during 1816–17.

While at Naples the ship was visited by the Emperor of Austria and the King of Naples. "Everything was in fine order on board," he writes, "and a grand display was made to entertain our illustrious guests. I acted as interpreter to the Emperor on that occasion. Prince Metternich was of the party, and I remember that he laughed at me during our tour around the ship for addressing the Emperor as 'mister.'" It might even be supposed that, with his characteristic sense of humor, Farragut was thus actually indulging in a sly joke at royalty's expense. At any rate, he proceeds to remark: "The Emperor was the only one of the party whose appearance struck me as ridiculous. He seemed to be a mere puppet, was attired in a white coat, with two loops of silk cord on each shoulder, buttoned to the collar, five large stars on his breast, and wore short, red breeches, with stockings and military boots. His cocked hat was decorated with a green plume, and he took short, mincing steps, presenting to my youthful mind altogether a silly appearance. The King of Naples was a tall, raw-boned, common-looking man."

VISIT OF THE EMPEROR OF AUSTRIA

Excessive reverence does not seem to have been a failing of Farragut's character at this time; he was also no admirer of the rigid and unreasonable notions of discipline then entertained in the navy, which several times in his experience, were made the subject of remonstrances to the Navy Department and Congress, and which, **NAVAL DISCIPLINE** he tells us, made the past-captains, "with the exception of a question of life and death, in the absolute authority they assumed, but little inferior to the Czar of all the Russias."

Nor does his sea-training seem to have been the best preparation in the world for a social favorite. When in Marseilles, in the winter of 1817, he made the acquaintance of an American family by the name of Fitch, and was several times entertained at their house. On one occasion, at a dinner party, he was, much against his inclination, obliged to play whist. "Not getting along very well with my hand," he says, "the party showed great impatience, and, I thought, were rather insulting in their remarks. One individual went so far as to dash his cards on the table in derision of my play, when I returned the compliment by throwing them at his head. I apologized to Mr. Fitch, and retired, much mortified, at being compelled to violate the proprieties of the occasion and the feelings of my host, but my temper had been sorely tried.''

While at Pisa, in 1818, he was invited to a ball given by the Countess Martioni in honor of the Grand Duke of Tuscany. Here again the display was by no means calculated to excite

A ROYAL BANQUET admiration in this singularly independent young officer. "We were shown into the supper-room," he says, "prepared for the Duke and his suite, and allowed to feast — our vision — on the table. . . . . We were permitted to walk around the table, and make our exit on the opposite side." During the evening he records such errors of his as treading on the Grand Duke's toe and catching his shoe-buckle in the flounce of the Archduchess' dress, and then, preparing to retire in confusion, only discovered his cocked hat extemporized into a foot-warmer by the Countess Testa. "I drew it to me rather unceremoniously," he says, "at which she remarked that I 'ought to feel myself highly complimented, and should not be offended.' To which I replied, 'Madam, it might be so considered in your country, but not in mine.'"

In the autumn of 1817, Reverend Charles Folsom, Chaplain of the "Washington," having

THE UNITED STATES FRIGATE "INDEPENDENCE."
(From a woodcut.)

been appointed United States Consul at Tunis, obtained leave of absence for the young midshipman in order that he might **RESIDENCE IN TUNIS** continue his studies, which constant sea-duty had seriously interrupted, and for nearly a year thereafter he resided at Tunis, perfecting his knowledge of modern

languages, literature and mathematics, also
traveling extensively in the Barbary States and
Southern Europe.   In December, 1818, he reported for duty at Messina, Sicily, where he spent
the remainder of the winter, and in the summer
of 1819 was appointed Acting-Lieutenant of the
brig "Shark."   This was his first position of
RETURN TO   actual authority, obtained be-
SERVICE   fore his twentieth year, and
nobly did his subsequent career verify his
theory that it is best to acquire command
when young, as a preparation for meeting the
responsibilities of active service.

After cruising in the Mediterranean for about
a year he was ordered home to pass examinations
for a full commission, and, finding no war ship
ready to sail for the United States, he took passage in the merchantman "America."   Within
a few days' sail of their destination they fell in
with a Colombian brig-of-war, and the captain,
supposing her to be a pirate, gave over the command to Farragut, who prepared to defend himself to the last extremity.   The ship's mission
proved to be merely a request to take charge of a
packet of letters, but the affair served well to dis-

play the young officer's prowess and cool-headedness. Passing his examination, none too well to suit his ambition, he was for about a year and a half stationed at Norfolk, Va. There he made the acquaintance of Miss Susan Marchant, daughter of Jordan Marchant, of Norfolk, to whom he was **MARRIAGE** married September 24, 1823. In May, 1822, he was ordered to the sloop-of-war "John Adams," which conveyed United States Minister Joel R. Poinsett to Mexico, and on his return was transferred to the schooner "Greyhound," of Commodore Porter's fleet, serving against the pirates in West Indian waters.

In the latter expedition he distinguished himself in several hazardous encounters, principally in command of landing parties, and through numerous romantic and exciting adventures succeeded in driving them from their haunts, and practically destroying some of their best bases of supply. He **SERVICE AGAINST PIRATES** also narrowly escaped the yellow fever, which carried off twenty-three out of the twenty-five officers who were stricken with the disease, and after a brief visit to his family at

New Orleans, again went to sea on the " Ferret."
On this ship, in July, 1823, he obtained his first
command, after some difficulty in overcoming
Commodore Porter's scruples against an appear-
FIRST ance of partiality and his rule
COMMAND fixing promotions by seniority
in service. During the next two years he was
mostly engaged in the duty of convoying merchant ships through the Gulf of Mexico, as a
guard against pirates.

He finally returned to Washington, where for
several weeks he was very ill with yellow fever,
and in August, 1825, shortly after his recovery,
he received the lieutenant's commission for which
he had vainly worked and waited during several
years. On this point he wittily remarks: " One
might suppose that these events of my life passed
lightly by; on the contrary, I had always to
contend with the burden first imposed on me by
Commodore Porter's saying that I was ' too young
for promotion.' Although that remark was made
just after the action of the ' Essex,' I never
SLOW appeared to get any older in
PROMOTION the eyes of the Government or
my Commander, and consequently had to con-

tend inch by inch, as opportunities presented, with men of riper age and apparently more entitled to the places sought. Still, my good star prevailed in this instance, and it is to the enjoyment of these trials that I have always felt myself indebted for whatever professional reputation I have attained."

Immediately after his promotion he was ordered to the frigate "Brandywine," Captain Charles Morris, which CRUISE ON THE "BRANDYWINE" had been designed to convey the Marquis de Lafayette to France. This ship, which was one of the fastest vessels in the world, made the voyage in twenty-five days, although she sprang a leak the first night out, thus necessitating the throwing overboard of 3,000 shot and some other stores. Upon his return in May, 1826, he located in New Haven, Conn., where his wife, a great sufferer from neuralgia, was placed under the care of an eminent specialist, and he himself attended lectures in Yale College. In the following October he was stationed on the receiving-ship "Alert," at Norfolk, where he continued for two years, meantime establishing and conducting a school for the naval apprentice

boys, many of whom did not know their letters.
He discovered in this work great ability as a
teacher, and his charges made such rapid progress
as to elicit from Secretary Southard, as he says,
"one of the few, the very few compliments I ever
received from the Navy Department or its head."

From October, 1828, to December, 1829, he
was Executive Officer of the sloop-of-war
VISIT TO "Vandalia," which cruised in
BRAZIL Brazilian waters during the revo-
lution culminating in the independence of the
Argentine Republic. He witnessed the festivities
incident upon the marriage of Emperor Dom
Pedro I., of Brazil, to his second wife, Donna
Amelia Augusta, daughter of Prince Eugene,
Duke of Leuchtenburg, and was presented at
court with other American officers.

Finally an affection of the eyes, due to a par-
tial sunstroke in Tunis in 1818, had so undermined his health that he was obliged to apply for
a furlough and return home for treatment, taking
passage on the brig "Barnegat," of Boston. Off
Cape St. Roque they were chased by a supposed
pirate craft, and by Farragut's direction mounted
their entire armament, four 18-pounder carron-

ades, while all hands "cut up their flannel shirts for cyliuders," aud prepared to give battle with "twenty-four pounds of powder and a quantity of musket balls and spike-nails." Fortunately the "Barnegat" out-sailed her pursuer, and the circumstance served only to furnish **AN UNFOUGHT BATTLE** a subject for conversation during the rest of the voyage.

After a passage of fifty days he arrived in Norfolk, where for the next seventeen months he was statioued on the receiving-ship "Congress." Iu August, 1831, he was ordered to the frigate "Java," and in December, 1831, transferred to the "Natchez," as Executive Officer with the full commission of a first lieutenant. He personally selected the crew of the "Natchez" from the receiving-ship, aud setting sail on January 2, 1833, ran into the port of Charleston, under orders to compel observance of the United States revenue laws, threatened by the South Carolina nullificationists. Their presence was, however, by **EXPEDITION TO CHARLES-TON, S. C.** no means hostilely construed, social events occupying most of the officers' time. Their boats were generally employed in taking company on board, and they entertained their visitors with music and dancing. On March 26th the ship set out on the return to Norfolk, arriving within a week with General Scott as a passenger, and after about one month's delay made sail for its new station on the coast of Brazil. At the end of about nine months, in course of which they had touched at Pernambuco, Bahia, Montevideo, Rio Janeiro and other ports, Farragut was transferred to the command of the schooner " Boxer," in which he started for home, June 8, 1834. On their arrival the ship was laid up, and her commander, being allowed a leave of absence on shore, was during the next four years on duty in every naval court-martial held at Norfolk.

From August 7, 1838, to January 12, 1839, he commanded the sloop " Erie," cruising along the Mexican coast, and witness-

THE FRANCO-MEXICAN WAR

ing such naval operations of the Franco-Mexican war as the blockade of the port of Vera Cruz and the fall of the supposedly impregnable Castle of San Juan de Ulloa, on which he made copious notes and observations. For two years thereafter, he was on land-fur-

lough, having no regular official duties outside of
naval court-martials, and literally devoted his
entire time to the care of his invalid wife until
her death, December 17, 1840. "No more
striking illustration of his gentleness of character
is shown," says his son, "than in Farragut's
attention to his invalid wife.
His tenderness in contributing to   **DEATH OF
MRS. FARRA-
GUT**
her every comfort, and catering
to every whim, through sixteen years of suffering, forms one of the brightest spots in the history of his domestic life." He further quotes the
remark of a lady of Norfolk that: "When
Captain Farragut dies, he should have a monu-
ment reaching to the skies made by every wife in
the city contributing a stone to it."

After the death of his wife, he again applied
for sea-service, and on February 22, 1841, received appointment as Executive Officer of the
"Delaware," in which he made another cruise
in Brazilian waters, being on his return, on September 27th following, commissioned commander. "I proceeded at once," he writes on
taking command, "to overhaul her and rig ship
with all possible dispatch," and his splendid sea-

manship was never better demonstrated than in
then devising a method of placing the half-tops
in about fifteen or twenty minutes, instead of

CRUISE TO SOUTH AMERICA from four hours to half a day, as previously. During his sojourn in South American waters he made numerous observations of interest, and among other notable characters met Juan Manuel de Rosas, the Argentine Dictator, in whose family he was repeatedly entertained. On June 1, 1842, he was transferred to the command of the "Decatur," and in November following set out on the return voyage, arriving at Norfolk, February 18, 1843. This cruise, under Commodore Morris, was one of great interest to the Navy; it was the first effort of the old officers to exercise in naval tactics by the squadron, almost abandoned since 1812.

On his return he went to Washington, and relates that Abel P. Upshur, then Secretary of the Navy, laughed at his "pretensions" for re-

FARRAGUT'S "PRETENSIONS" taining command of the "Decatur," which was destined for the coast of Africa. This method of treating efficient officers in the service may

FARRAGUT LASHED TO THE RIGGING OF THE "HART
FORD" DURING THE BATTLE OF MOBILE BAY.

have been perfectly usual; Farragut's abilities
may have been underrated, or his sensibilities
over keen, yet his journal abounds in complaints
of the injustice done him by his superiors,
whom, in turn, he freely criticizes. In April,
1844, he was appointed Executive Officer of the
" Pennsylvania," of which he later became Commander, succeeding Captain Smoot, and was
then made Second Officer of the Norfolk Navy
Yard, under Commander Wilkinson. The outbreak of the Mexican War found him again
making application for a command, urging as

**OPENING OF
THE MEXICAN
WAR**

a ground of fitness for active
service his previous experience in
Gulf waters and among Spanish
peoples. " I urged," he says, " that I could take
the Castle of San Juan with the ' Pennsylvania '
and two sloops of war like the ' Saratoga,' for
which declaration I came very near being ruled
out as a monomaniac. I was willing to take the
inferior position of Executive Officer on board the
' Pennsylvania,' that I might have the duty of
organizing her crew for the fight; but it was
not permitted, and I did not obtain command
of the ' Saratoga ' until February, 1847."

Taken as a whole, it is not remarkable that
Farragut calls this cruise the most mortifying in
his experience. He arrived in time to find the
castle in the hands of the army instead of
the navy, and, animadverting severely on the
misleading statement of an Eng- **A MORTIFY-**
lish officer, that "the castle **ING SERVICE**
could sink all the ships in the world,"
proceeds to remark that as a result of miss-
ing an unprecedented opportunity, "not one
of the officers concerned will ever wear an admiral's flag." Added to this annoyance, he
nearly died of yellow fever, and, having had a
clash with Commodore M. C. Perry, was assigned
to obscure and inglorious duties. He finally
petitioned to be relieved of his command, and
reaching New York after about one year's
absence, was returned to his former position
in the Norfolk Navy Yard.

In October, 1850, with four other officers, he
was ordered to draw up a book of ordnance reg-
ulations for the navy—a task which occupied in
all eighteen months. Greatly to his disgust,
many of the best features were overruled and
stricken out, as were also the drawings, which

they considered fine illustrations. " Those who had the power," he writes, " called a new board

BOOK ON NAVAL ORDNANCE

ten years after, and made a few necessary changes to suit the introduction of steam and heavy guns, and the names of the original board were obliterated. . . . I do not care for the praise that such a volume might win, but I despise the spirit that prompts those who have a little temporary power about the seat of government to purloin the credit due to others."

In 1854 he petitioned for an appointment as United States representative to observe the naval operations of the Crimean War, but instead he was assigned to the duty of establishing a navy yard at Mare Island, in San Pablo Bay, Cal. There he remained until July, 1858,

SERVICES IN CALIFORNIA

devoting his energies to the work and strictly refraining from interference of any kind in local affairs. By this wise policy he maintained the strict neutrality of the Federal Government in the troubles following the high-handed acts of the vigilance committee of 1856, and thus, likely, saved the State from the horrors of civil war.

At the end of his term of appointment he was summoned home and assigned to the newly-completed cruiser "Brooklyn," which he commanded on her trial trip, and later on an extended cruise in the Gulf of Mexico, conveying United States Minister Robert M. McLane to various points along the coast, as his official duties led him. When accused of having thus consented to be at the beck of a "mere civilian," he replied, characteristically, that he "would rather be subject to the directions of an intelligent man appointed by the Government, for a purpose, and on account of his qualifications, than

**CRUISE
IN THE
"BROOKLYN"**

to be under some old fool whose only merit was that he had been in the navy all his life." Yet the Government's action in similarly placing a junior officer over him, when the "Brooklyn" was designated to convey an exploring party for a proposed route across the Isthmus of Chiriqui, met with his prompt and vigorous resentment. He was accordingly relieved in October, 1860, and returning from Aspinwall to Norfolk, remained on waiting orders until the outbreak of the Civil War.

Although a Southerner by birth and by all the
ties of blood and friendship, his loyalty to the
Old Flag under which he had served so long made
him, through all the period of Secessionist agita-
tion, a firm opponent of the armed resistance he
foresaw as inevitable. On the other hand, as has
been stated, a peaceable withdrawal of the
Southern States would likely have found him
among his friends. " God forbid," was his constant prayer, "that I should raise my hand

**LOYALTY TO
THE UNION** against the South." Yet when
Virginia passed the Ordinance
of Secession, and the forts and arsenals were
seized, he openly declared that President
Lincoln was fully justified in calling for troops.
The imminent estrangement from all his
associates consequent on his loyalist opinions
led him to remove from Norfolk on April 19,
1861, and thereafter, until the close of the war,
his family resided at Hastings-on-Hudson. In
this quiet retreat he himself remained for nearly
a year, seeing no official service save on the Naval
Retiring Board convened in Brooklyn.

Meantime his energetic spirit chafed with
impatience at enforced idleness when there

was work doing for his country, and, while
eagerly awaiting his turn, he petitioned the
Government for a command to   **OBTAINS**
follow and overtake the Con-   **COMMAND**
federate cruiser "Sumter," regarding the move-
ments of which he had very well-defined ideas.
The Government, however, was already con-
sidering the advisability of appointing him to
a much wider field—the command of the pro-
jected Western Gulf Blockading Squadron.
Finally, on January 9, 1862, he was officially
informed of his appointment to this important trust, and on February 2d he sailed on
the steam sloop "Hartford" from Hampton
Roads, arriving at the appointed · rendezvous,
Ship Island, in seventeen days.

His fleet, consisting of six war steamers, sixteen gunboats, twenty-one mortar-vessels, under
command of Commander David   **THE GULF**
D. Porter, and five supply   **SQUADRON**
ships, was the largest that had ever sailed
under the American flag. Yet the task assigned him, the passing of the forts below New
Orleans, the capture of the city, and the opening
of the Mississippi River through its entire length,

was one of difficulty unprecedented in the history
of naval warfare. Arrived at the mouth of the
river, the real work began in the attempt to
force an entrance over the bar with the larger
vessels of his squadron. One, the "Colorado,"
drawing twenty-two feet of water, had to be left
outside; and three others, the "Brooklyn,"
"Pensacola," and "Mississippi," were towed
with great delay and labor through a foot of mud.
Meantime, on April 8th, Captain Gerdes had, by

IN THE MISSISSIPPI RIVER Farragut's orders, made a complete triangulation of the river
shore below the forts, and on the
13th, the mortar schooners, their masts dressed
with bushes to conceal their positions behind the
thick woods, opened fire on the fortifications.
After over a week of steady work, in course of
which nearly 16,000 shells were thrown, no appre-
ciable damage was done to the defences of the
enemy, nor were any of his guns silenced. Farragut's distrust of the mortar service seemed fully
justified by this result, as in his opinion they had
served only to warn the Confederates of the im-
pending attack, and during the delay the other
vessels of his fleet had suffered much from the

swiftness of the current, several of them parting their anchor cables and incurring considerable damage by collision. Several fire-rafts—flat-boats piled high with pitch-pine timber and ig-nited—had also been sent down the river, but by

THE UNITED STATES STEAM SLOOP "HARTFORD."

constant watchfulness all had either been grap-pled and beached or had floated harmlessly out to sea.

In this period of delay he employed the time in closely inspecting and preparing his vessels for the contemplated ascent of the river, and issued orders, which were most precise and care-fully considered, for meeting every possible emergency. The heavy chain stretched across the river between Fort Jackson and the eastern

A GALLANT EXPLOIT shore was cut amid a storm of shot and shell in the night of April 21st by Captain Henry H. Bell, and even during his engrossing tasks Farragut found time to feel anxiety for his lieutenant, writing in his journal shortly after: "I was as glad to see Bell on his return as if he had been my boy. I was up all night and could not sleep until he got back to the ship."

At last, shortly before 4 o'clock on the morning of April 24th, the squadron set out on its hazardous attempt to pass the forts that had in 1815 defied the British for nine days, and even at that late date were considered impassable. The attack was made in two columns; the right led by Captain Theodorus Bailey, with eight vessels, including the "Cayuga," "Pensacola" and "Mississippi," and the left, by Farragut, with the "Hartford," "Brooklyn," "Richmond" and six

THE FLEET PASSES UP THE RIVER others, while Porter brought up the rear with six gunboats, under orders to take up a position where he could pour in an enfilading fire while the others passed the forts. The first of the ships had scarcely passed the hulks supporting the severed chain across the stream when both forts—Jackson and St. Philip—opened on her with a furious fire. Meantime Porter's mortars had opened on Fort Jackson from below, and the two divisions of Farragut's fleet, so soon as the works were in range, began pouring in grape and canister. Amid the deafening thunder of over two hundred guns they moved steadily on at full steam, the signal '' close action '' blazing from the '' Hartford's '' main-top. "The white smoke rose and heaved in vast volumes along the shud-

THE PASSAGE OF THE FORTS

dering waters, and one of the wildest scenes in the history of war had now commenced. . . . Louder than redoubled thunders the heavy guns sent their deafening roar through the gloom, not in distinct explosions, but in one long, wild, protracted crash, as though the ribs of nature were breaking in final convulsion.''

After passing beyond the range of St. Philip, Captain Bailey's division engaged in a desperate encounter with the eleven Confederate gunboats, which were destroyed one after another amid

prodigies of valor on both sides.   But one Federal
vessel, the " Varuna," was lost, although three
others were so badly damaged as to turn back and
float helplessly down the river.   The greatest loss
of life (thirty-seven) occurred on the " Pensacola," while the " Hartford," " Cayuga " and
" Brooklyn " escaped as by a miracle from the
gravest dangers.   At one time the " Hartford "
ran aground, and was set on fire by a fire-raft
A GLORIOUS   pushed against her by the ram
VICTORY   " Manassas," only the coolness
of the commander and the perfect discipline
of the crew saving her from certain destruction.   The " Manassas " was almost immediately after riddled by a broadside from the
" Mississippi," and then boarded and set on fire,
she drifted down the current and blew up opposite
Fort Jackson.   " When the sun struggled up
through the morning mist," says Headley, " he
looked down on a scene never to be forgotten
while naval deeds are honored by the nation.
There lay the forts with the rebel flag still flying,
but their doom was sealed.   And there, driven
ashore or wrecked or captured were the enemy's
gunboats, which had been brought down to assist

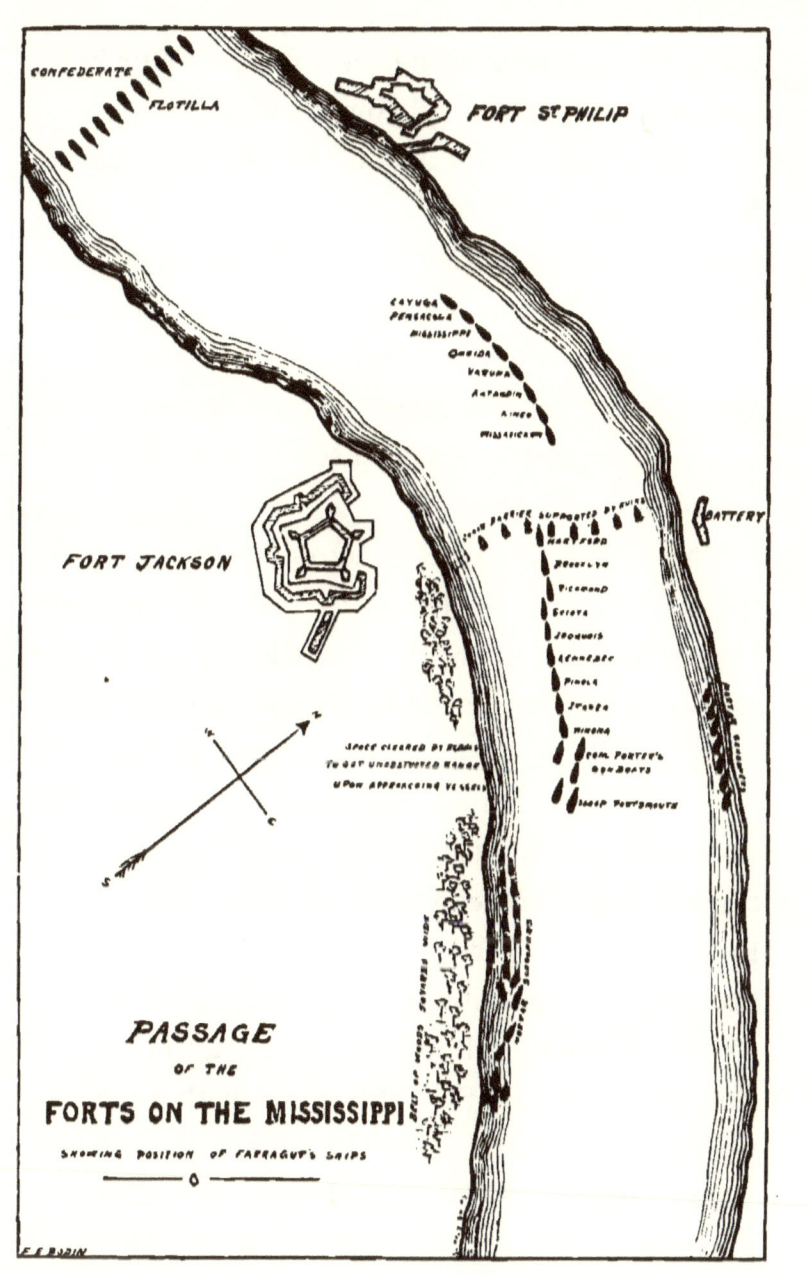

CONFEDERATE
FLOTILLA

FORT St PHILIP

CAYUGA
PENSACOLA
MISSISSIPPI
ONEIDA
VARUNA
KATAHDIN
KINEO
WISSAHICKON

BATTERY

PICKETS SUPPORTED BY BU...
HARTFORD
BROOKLYN
RICHMOND
SCIOTA
IROQUOIS
KENNEBEC
PINOLA
ITASCA
WINONA
COM PORTER'S
GUN BOATS
USS PORTSMOUTH

FORT JACKSON

SPACE CLEARED BY FLAMES
TO GET UNOBSTRUCTED RANGE
UPON APPROACHING VESSELS

PASSAGE
OF THE
FORTS ON THE MISSISSIPPI
SHOWING POSITION OF FARRAGUT'S SHIPS

F.E. BODIN

the forts in demolishing our fleet." Our total
loss in this unparalleled combat was 171.

Captain John Wilkinson, of the Confederate
Navy, in speaking of this surprising feat, says:
" Most of us belonging to that little naval fleet
knew that Admiral Farragut would dare to attempt what any man would," but all authorities
agree that " had the passage been attempted in
broad daylight the Union fleet would have sus-
tained a fearful loss."

The importance of the victory was very great ;
its immediate result being to prevent Napoleon
III. from recognizing the Confederacy and taking
steps to raise the blockade, as had been his inten-
IMPORTANT RESULTS tion.   Continuing at once to
New   Orleans,   Farragut de-
manded its immediate surrender, and after
several days of vexatious correspondence with
the Mayor, he raised the Stars and Stripes again
above the custom house and city hall.   This victory was closely followed by the capitulation of
Forts Jackson and St. Philip, and within a week
the forces under General Butler had occupied
New Orleans.   At this time Farragut's desire was
to proceed at once to attack Mobile, Ala., and

he hence abandonded his contemplated assault on the strong defenses of Vicksburg, Miss., and returned to New Orleans. There he received orders to continue in the Mississippi until the river was opened to the Federal fleet through its entire length. He accordingly pro- ceeded to Vicksburg, taking **ATTACK ON VICKSBURG** Grand Gulf in passing, and, having run by the batteries, joined Commodore Charles H. Davis' fleet of ironclads above the city. The expedition failed, however, from non-support by the land forces, and on July 15th he again ran past the city on his way down the river.

On the following day, July 16, 1862, in recognition of Farragut's exceptional services, Congress created the rank of rear-admiral for his express benefit—the title of ad- miral having hitherto been un- **UNPRECE-DENTED HONORS** known in the United States Navy —and, as though the most exalted honors had been providentially reserved to reward his unprecedented gallantry, he was the first to receive the title of vice-admiral on December 23, 1864, and of admiral on July 25, 1866.

The remainder of the year 1862 was passed in

the river, with small engagements at various
points, and the capture of such strongholds as
Corpus Christi, Sabine Pass and Galveston, and
when arrangements had been perfected for co-
operation of the land and naval forces, early

THE FALL OF PORT HUDSON in 1863, Farragut once more returned to the task of reducing
Vicksburg. On March 14, 1863,
with two ships he succeeded in running the
gauntlet of the batteries at Port Hudson, four
miles in extent ; all his other vessels suffering
severely in the attempt, and the fine frigate
" Mississippi " having run aground, was blown
up by her commander.   With the " Hartford "
and "Albatross" he blockaded the mouth of the
Red River for over two months, effectually cut-
ting off the Confederate supplies, and later co-
operated with General Banks in the investment
of Port Hudson, assisting in its capture on July
9th.

After about five months in New York, awaiting
the refitting of his ships, he returned to the
command of the Gulf Squadron, and in the
following summer completed his preparations to
co-operate with General Gordon Granger in the

capture of Mobile. On August 5, 1864, he steamed past the batteries in the Bay to a point directly opposite the city, thus repeating in daring and brilliancy his achievements in the Mississippi below New Orleans over two years before. It was in this fight, and after the sinking of the ironclad "Tecumseh," which ran foul of a submarine mine and went down with almost her entire crew, that Farragut, lashed to the rigging of the "Hartford," gave orders to put his vessel in the van of the fleet.* The coolness and determination of this manœuvre, executed in a scathing fire in defiance of the greatest danger from torpedoes and other obstructions, inspired the whole fleet with confidence, and ensured the victory.

THE BATTLE OF MOBILE BAY

---

* The officer who lashed Farragut to the rigging of the "Hartford" was Lieutenant John Crittenden Watson, now (1899) Rear-Admiral and successor of Dewey in command of the U. S. Squadron in Manila Bay. In a letter, written to his mother at the time, Watson describes his act in these words : "At length I lashed him to the rigging with my own hands, having in vain begged him not to stand in such an exposed place" Between the young lieutenant and his gallant commander there seems to have been a close and affectionate regard, and Farragut specially mentions him in his report on the Battle of Mobile for bravery and faithful attention to duty.

As at New Orleans, the Confederate fleet was entirely destroyed, even including the ram "Tennessee," which, defying the fire of the fleet and menacing the flag-ship with destruction, was

RUNNING THE FORTS IN MOBILE BAY.

finally compelled to surrender by the monitors with their terrible Dahlgren guns.*   One of the

---

* The Dahlgren guns, so called from their distinguished inventor Rear-Admiral Charles Adolph Dahlgren, are historic, not only in the fact that they furnished the model and impetus for modern naval armaments, but also for their wonderful part in saving the integrity of the Federal Union.   They were many strides in advance of anything that preceded them, in scientific principles of construction, accuracy, power, and endurance ; they necessitated iron-clad ships, and also set a period to the old theories of land fortification.   Their distinctive feature was a great thickness at the breach, with the barrel rapidly tapering from the trunnions to the muzzle—"soda water bottles" they were called—adjusted to meet the varying pressure of the explosive force.

In an able paper on the Dahlgren guns, the admiral's son, Charles

forts, Fort Morgan, held out for three days, but Farragut's dash had rendered resistance useless, and actually crushed the last hope of the Confederates in Gulf waters.

Shortly after this achievement he was relieved

Bunker Dahlgren, enumerates nine important engagements in the Civil War in which they turned the tide of success: at Port Royal, S. C., November 6, 1861, where the frigate "Wabash," with her forty Dahlgren guns, silenced the forts and secured a harbor for the Federal Fleet; at the attack on Forts Jackson and St. Philip, April 24, 1862, when the fleet under Farragut and Porter destroyed the Confederate rams and earthworks; at the battle between the United States monitor "Weehawken," and the Confederate iron-clad "Atlanta," June 17, 1863, when the two Dahlgren guns of the former crushed in the sides of the enemy in twenty-six minutes; at the blockade of Charleston harbor, when Dahlgren guns not only silenced the forts, but put an effectual stop to blockade running; during the siege of Vicksburg, May-July, 1863, when the heavy Dahl-grens loaned by Admiral Porter, accomplished the silencing of the forts in four days; at the battle between the "Kearsarge" and "Alabama," July 19, 1864, when the two XI-inch Dahlgrens of the Federal ship sunk the enemy in fifty-nine minutes; at Farragut's attack on Mobile, in August, 1864, when the formidable ram "Tennessee," a terror to ships of every class, was destroyed by the steady fire of the monitors "Manhattan" and "Chickasaw"; at Fort Fisher, January 15, 1865, "where the roar from the crescent of Dahlgren guns of Admiral Porter's fleet resembled Niagara, and their precision of fire was wonderful, knocking the Confederate guns quickly out of existence, as well as the gunners." The most memorable occasion of their use, however, was at the battle of Hampton Roads, between the "Monitor" and "Virginia" ("Merrimac"), when the two XI-inch Dahlgrens of the former gained the day, and saved the Federal fleet from destruction. Commenting on this engagement, Admiral David D. Porter writes: "I was the first person who ever fired the XI-inch Dahlgren with thirty pounds of powder, and am of the opinion that, had the 'Monitor' used that charge the 'Merrimac' would have been captured."

of his command at his own request, and in December was given a grand ovation in New York City, and a gift of $50,000 to purchase a house there.   Later he accepted a temporary command

ENCOUNTER BETWEEN THE "HARTFORD" AND "TENNESSEE."

in the James River, Virginia, where he was stationed at the time of the fall of Richmond.

In 1868 Admiral Farragut sailed from Brooklyn in the frigate " Franklin," and commanded the European Squadron for about a year. During this period he visited many of the countries of Europe, and touched at several stations in Asia and Africa, being received with distinguished honor by rulers and people wherever he landed. The Sultan of Turkey accorded him a privilege previously reserved exclusively for royalty—permitting him to pass the Dardanelles in a war-ship. Shortly after his return from this trip, failing health compelled his retirement from active service.

Admiral Farragut's was an exceptional character, not only in its strength, but also in its gentleness and deep feeling. His religious faith was childlike and sincere. In his family life he was **FARRAGUT'S NOBLE CHARACTER** the indulgent father and the devoted husband ; on ship-board the stern disciplinarian, and yet the beloved commander of the humblest sailor. One of his fellow-officers wrote when Farragut was executive officer of the "Natchez" (1833): "Never was the crew of a man-of-war better disciplined or more contented and happy. The moment all hands were called and Farragut took the trumpet, every man under him was alive and eager for duty." After the terrible fight in Mobile Bay, it is related that Farragut, old though he was in the ways of war, shed tears "like a little child," as his Quartermaster puts it, on seeing the mangled dead and wounded bodies that had paid the price of his great victory.

The Admiral was married for the second time to Virginia, daughter of William Loyall, of Norfolk, Va., on December 26, 1843, and had one son, Loyall Farragut.

He died at Portsmouth, N. H., Aug. 14, 1870, and his remains lie in Woodlawn Cemetery, New York City.

An excellent biography has been written by his son (New York, 1879), and another by Joel T. Headley. A statue of him by St. Gaudens adorns Madison Square, New York, and another by Vinnie Ream is in Farragut Square, Washington, D. C

A CIVIL WAR MONITOR.

(From a wartime woodcut.)

DAVID D. PORTER

David D Porter

PORTER

DAVID DIXON PORTER, the second Admiral of the United States Navy, was born at Chester, Pa., June 8, 1813. He came of a family that through several generations had been conspicuous for sea-service. His great-grandfather, Alexander Porter, for many years previous to the Revolution, commanded a merchant ship sailing from the port of Boston, and gave valuable **A SEAFARING FAMILY** aid to the colonies in the early stages of the struggle. His grandfather, David Porter, commanded one of the vessels commissioned by General Washington to intercept British supply ships, forming the nucleus of the American Navy. He afterward commanded the "Delight," six guns, and the "Aurora," ten guns, fitted out by the Americans; and toward the end of the war was appointed sailing-master in the Navy, a post filled by him until his death

at New Orleans in 1808. Both his sons, John
and David, were early inured to the hardships

of a sailor's life;
the former died
in 1831, having
risen to the rank
of commander.

David Porter,
father of the
Admiral, was
one of the most
famous of early
American naval
heroes.   He be-
gan his career in 1798 under Captain Thomas
Truxtun, receiving honorable mention and an

**DAVID
PORTER**

award for bravery in his first
battle, that between the "Constellation" and "l'Insurgente," and being commissioned lieutenant before his twentieth year.
In the war with Tripoli he rendered notable
service as commander of a boat expedition detailed to destroy shipping, but was captured on
the frigate "Philadelphia," in October, 1803,
and held captive until the close of the war.

His most memorable exploit, however, was his voyage to the Pacific in the "Essex" (1813-14), in course of which he inflicted untold harm on the British shipping, and nearly destroyed their whaling interests in southern waters. Arriving on January 12, 1814, in the harbor of Valparaiso, Chili, he was blockaded there for over six weeks by the British frigates "Cherub" and "Phœbe," and finally attempting to escape on March 28th, was forced into combat with both vessels. This action was one of the most

THE UNITED STATES FRIGATE "ESSEX."

gallant of the war. Porter continued the fight for two hours and a half, until his ship was literally shot to pieces. All but 75

of his crew of 225 were killed or disabled,
and no alternative was left but to surrender.

In his report to the Navy Department he said: " We have been
unfortunate but not disgraced."
And in view of the fact that to have chosen
rather to go down with colors flying would
have involved the destruction of scores of
helpless wounded heroes, the remark seems
eminently just.   Although the " Essex " was
nearly unmanageable, he attempted to board his
adversaries three times, only to expose himself to severe rakings; he also failed in the effort
to run her aground.   His heroism excited the
admiration even of his enemies.

In 1823, being placed in command of a special
expedition sent against West Indian pirates, he
added to his already great reputation, driving
them from nearly all their haunts, and destroying or capturing large numbers of their vessels.
Finally, having received information of a pirate
rendezvous at Foxardo, Porto Rico, he dispatched
one of his fleet, the " Beagle," to investigate
the report.   On landing, her commander was
thrown into prison by the Spanish authorities

on the charge of being a pirate himself, and
Commodore Porter, arriving
somewhat later, demanded a
AN INSULT
TO THE FLAG
prompt apology for this insult to the United
States flag. In this affair the Navy Department judged that he had exceeded his authority and violated the recognized principles
of international law, but in recognition of his
zeal in defence of the flag, the court-martial
called to investigate the case, recommended
clemency. He was sentenced to suspension for
six months. This unnecessarily severe treatment so nettled him that he resigned his commission, and, in August, 1826, accepted the
proffered position of Commander-in-chief in the
navy of Mexico, then engaged in her struggle for
independence.

Later he was appointed United States Consul
to the Barbary States, and from 1831 until his
death was *chargé d'affaires* at Constantinople. He
wrote two books, '' Journal of a Cruise Made to
the Pacifick Ocean by the U. S. Frigate ' Essex,' ''
illustrated with his own sketches (1822), and
'' Constantinople and its Environs '' (1835). He
died on his estate, '' San Stefano,'' at Pera, a

suburb of Constantinople, Turkey, March 3,
1843. His remains were brought to the United
States on the brig-of-war "Truxtun," and lie
buried in Philadelphia.

Commodore Porter trained the two illustrious
men who first held the rank of admiral in the
United States Navy—his son, David D. Porter,
and his foster-son, David G. Farragut—and
indelibly stamped his own remarkable traits on
the characters of both. He had six sons:

A NOTABLE FAMILY William David, Theodoric, Hamilton, Thomas, David Dixon and
Henry Ogden Porter. Thomas and Hamilton
died early. Theodoric was the first American
army officer killed in the Mexican War, falling
in 1846 in an engagement with the enemy's
cavalry near Fort Brown, on the Rio Grande,
while serving on a scouting expedition as Second
Lieutenant of the 4th Infantry. Henry Ogden
entered the United States Navy in 1840;
resigned in 1847, and served with General
William Walker in one of his expeditions to
Central America ; was later attached to the
United States Revenue Marine, and was Executive of the " Hatteras," when she was sunk by

the Confederate steamer "Alabama." He died in Baltimore, Md., in 1869.

William David Porter, the eldest of the family, entered the Navy in 1823. On the outbreak of the Civil War he was assigned to duty in the Western Department under Commodore Foote, and, being placed
in command of a St. Louis ferry-
boat, was ordered to transform her into a gun-

WILLIAM
DAVID
PORTER

boat within eighteen days. The result was one of the most formidable vessels used in the Civil War; her sides were protected by a solid timber shield two feet thick, and her armament included two 9-inch and one 10-inch Dahlgrens. She was named "Essex," and in her victorious career she nobly rivaled the old frigate of the War of 1812.

His first important fight was at Columbus, Ky., the highest point on the Mississippi River fortified by the Confederates, where he put to flight three steamers that were attempting to tow a battery up the river. Later, in the attack on Fort Henry, the "Essex" proved an efficient aid to Foote's fleet, maintaining a terrific fire and dismounting many of the Confederate guns, until a 32-pound shot entered one of her portholes, penetrating the boiler, and causing a terrific overflow of steam, which killed or seriously disabled twenty-nine officers and men. Captain Porter

THE UNITED STATES GUNBOAT "ESSEX."

himself was severely scalded, at first supposed to be fatally, and his eyesight was impaired for several months. On July 13th, 1862, he rejoined the Squadron before Vicksburg, and there, on the morning of the 22d, under the guns of the forts, attacked, single-handed, the formidable ram "Arkansas," which had, some days previously defied the broadsides of the entire Federal fleet. Steaming close to this monster he literally

CAREER OF THE "ESSEX."

"tore up her iron-plating as if it had been nothing but so much pine lumber," but then retreated, unwilling to expose his vessel to the fire of the shore batteries. On the 6th of the succeeding month, after partici- pating with two other gunboats at Baton Rouge, he again re-

DEFEAT OF THE "ARKAN- SAS"

turned to engage her, this time completing her destruction by a steady fire of his 9-inch battery, driving her ashore and setting her on fire.

Captain Porter gave timely notice to the Washington authorities that the Confederates intended to fortify Port Hudson, and through the ignoring of his information many hundreds of lives were sacrificed. Later he assisted at the capitulation of Vicksburg.

The arduous service of several years had so undermined his constitution that he was relieved from duty at his own request, and going to New

DEATH OF COMMODORE PORTER

York for medical treatment, died there, in St. Luke's Hospital, May 1, 1864. Just previous to his resignation he was created Commodore by special order of President Lincoln.

David Dixon Porter, the youngest but one of

this illustrious family, served continuously for sixty-two years in the United States Navy, and attained a higher rank than any other officer, excepting only David G. Farragut. True to hereditary traditions, he went to sea at a very

BOYHOOD OF THE ADMIRAL

early age, serving with his father when but eleven years old in the expedition against the West Indian pirates. Two years later, when Commodore Porter joined the Mexican Navy, he secured a midshipman's commission for his son David, and the lad served throughout the Spanish War under his first cousin, Captain David H. Porter, who had also joined the Mexicans. His career in this service, however, lasted but a little more than a year. It came to an end when Captain Porter, in the armed brig "Guerrero," attacked off the coast of Cuba two Spanish warships which were convoying a fleet of merchant vessels. The smoke and din of the conflict brought to the aid of the Spaniards the

HIS FIRST BATTLE.

"Lealtad," a 64-gun frigate and after a desperate fight, in which Captain Porter and eighty of his men were killed, the "Guerrero" was forced to

strike her colors. The fourteen-year-old midshipman was taken prisoner and confined in the
guardship at Havana, but he was soon released
and permitted to return to the States.

On February 2, 1829, he was commissioned a
midshipman in the United States Navy, and assigned to the frigate "Constellation" of the Mediterranean Squadron. He was later attached to the
"United States" and the "Delaware" on the
same station. He was promoted IN THE U. S.
passed midshipman, July 3, 1835, NAVY
and from 1837 to 1840 was attached to the United
States Coast Survey. He was commissioned
lieutenant, February 27, 1841; during 1843-45
was once more with the Mediterranean Squadron,
on the frigate "Congress;" and after spending
part of the year 1846 at the Naval Observatory,
Washington, D. C., was dispatched to San Domingo, as Special Commissioner of the State
Department.

On the outbreak of the Mexican War he was
assigned to recruiting duty at New Orleans, and
in February, 1847, was detailed to the steamer
"Spitfire," Captain Josiah Tattnall. This ship,
with the "Vixen" and two small gunboats, was

selected by Commodore Perry to bombard the
forts of Vera Cruz, opposite Castle San Juan de
Ulloa, and after six hours' firing succeeded in
effecting considerable damage in the city. Under
cover of the night, Lieutenant Porter approached
the shore in a small boat to take soundings, and
next morning piloted the little flotilla nearer
shore, where a fierce encounter with the batteries
of the Castle ensued.

Porter served on the "Spitfire" in the expedition against Tuspan, and the fortifications on the
HIS FIRST   river banks above the city. In
COMMAND   the attack on Fort Iturbide,
above the city of Tobasco, June 16, 1847, at the
head of a detachment of sixty-eight men he
landed, charged and captured the works, holding
them securely until the arrival of Commodore
Perry, five hours later, after a weary march of sixteen miles from a point of landing below the city.
For this service he was placed in command of
the "Spitfire," and during the remainder of the
war figured in every action along the Gulf Coast
of Mexico.

During 1848-49 he was again attached to the
Coast Survey, but, having obtained a leave of

absence in 1850, he commanded mail steamers plying between New York and the Isthmus of Darien for four years. Among his exploits at this period was running the steamer "Crescent City" into the harbor of Ha- **AN** vana during the excitement in **ENCOUNTER WITH** relation to the ship "Black **SPANIARDS** Warrior." The Spanish Government had refused to permit any United States vessel to enter that port, but running directly under the shotted guns of Morro Castle, Porter, when ordered to halt replied that he carried the United States flag and the United States mail and was determined to enter the harbor of Havana. This he was permitted to do, the Spaniards thinking it not prudent to fire upon him. In 1855–57 he commanded the store-ship "Supply," and in 1858–60 was attached to the navy yard at Portsmouth, N. H.

When the Civil War seemed immediately imminent, David D. Porter, still a lieutenant, was summoned to **FORT** Washington for consultation on **PICKENS OCCUPIED** securing possession of Fort Pickens, at Pensacola, Fla., and was placed in command of the steamer

" Powhatan," to accomplish this duty. The occupation of the fort was effected without firing a shot, and the place was secured against Confederate attacks within twenty-four hours. He, however, sent two shells into the navy yard, and dislodged the Confederate garrison. These were

FIRST GUNS OF THE CIVIL WAR the first hostile guns fired by the United States Navy in the Civil War, three days after the fall of Sumter. On the same day he was promoted commander.

He was then sent in pursuit of the Confederate cruiser " Sumter," which was making havoc of American shipping in West Indian waters, and, having chased her 10,000 miles in vain, returned home.

While blockading the Southwest Pass of the Mississippi Delta, he conceived the idea of entering the river and capturing New Orleans, and on his return to Washington suggested the plan to

PLAN TO CAPTURE NEW ORLEANS Secretary Welles. So favorably was the department impressed with his representations that he might easily have gained command of the expedition, but he himself proposed Farragut for the post, and after having convinced the authorities of his loyalty and fitness for the command, despite his Southern birth, was dispatched to New York to offer it to him. Farragut's answer was : " I will take it if you go along "—a proposition which Porter accepted with delight. He, accordingly,

MORTAR VESSELS IN THE MISSISSIPPI.

joined the fleet with twenty-one schooners, each carrying a 13-inch mortar, and the whole convoyed by five war steamers. General Benjamin F. Butler was given command of the co-operating land forces. With this mortar fleet, Porter, in the spring of 1862, made his memorable attack

on Forts Jackson and St. Philip, the river defences of New Orleans. For six days and nights
he bombarded the forts, discharging at them no
less than 16,800 shells. Then occurred the
famous river fight and the running of the forts by
Farragut, closely followed by the capitulation of
New Orleans. Four days later, on April 28th,
the forts surrendered to Porter and his mortar
flotilla.

Commenting on the news of this successful
issue, Secretary Welles wrote to Porter: "The
important part which you have borne in the or-
ganization of the mortar flotilla,
and the movement on New Orleans, has identified your name
with one of the most brilliant naval achievements
on record; and to your able assistance with the
flotilla is Flag-Officer Farragut much indebted
for the successful results he has accomplished."

OFFICIAL COMMENDA-TION

The next conspicuous service of Commander
Porter was in the operations upon the Mississippi
between New Orleans and Vicksburg. His bombardment of the Vicksburg forts enabled Farragut to pass them, and he says in his report of
June 30, 1862: "The mortar flotilla has never

done better service than at Vicksburg." In
September, 1862, he received command of the
Mississippi squadron as acting rear-admiral; the
fleet having been increased from twelve vessels
to many times that number by furnishing the
ordinary river steamers with
guns and protective armor. **COMMANDER IN THE MISSISSIPPI**
Early in 1863, with eight of
these vessels, Porter co-operated with General
Sherman in the reduction of Arkansas Post,
silencing the fire of the fort and pounding the
bomb-proofs into fragments. The fort finally
surrendered to him; the Confederate army of
5,000 men, lying outside the works, to General
Sherman. He received his first vote of thanks
from Congress for this service.

On the night of April 16th, in the same year,
he ran the Vicksburg batteries with his fleet, and
although every one of his ships was struck, none
of them was materially damaged. Being then
south of Vicksburg he attacked, **ATTACK ON VICKSBURG**
in conjunction with General
Grant, the enemy's works at Grand Gulf, bring-
ing to bear against them eighty-one pieces of
artillery, and silencing their batteries. On the

surrender of Vicksburg, July 4, 1863, after a siege of five months, he again received the thanks of Congress and the commission of rear-admiral, to date from the day of the capitulation.

In the Spring of 1864 he co-operated with General Banks in the combined Army and Navy expedition against the strongholds along the

FEDERAL GUNBOATS IN THE RED RIVER.

Red River, in order to open the surrounding country as a base of supplies. The time was **RED RIVER EXPEDITION** chosen to take advantage of the spring freshets, and they actually penetrated as far west as Alexandria, La. There, on account of the subsidence of the stream, the larger gunboats were literally unable to proceed or return. At the advice of the army engineers, Porter was reluctantly preparing to burn his fleet, when the genius of Lieutenant-Colonel Joseph Bailey, a simple Wisconsin farmer, conceived the daring project of building a dam to deepen the water in mid-channel, and thus allow their escape. His proposition was condemned, but being finally adopted, was successfully accomplished. Three thousand men, kept at work night and day, constructed dams on either side of the river, leaving a stream sixty-five feet wide, which permitted the safe passage of all the fleet.

The expedition was a total failure through the incompetence and dilatory policy of General Banks, who suffered a severe defeat at the hands of General Thomas Green, and would probably have been annihilated but for Porter's timely appearance with his gunboats. Flushed with victory the Confederates boldly attacked the Federal fleet, calculating that the lofty banks of the river, the low water, and the grounding of most of the vessels would enable them to make short work of Porter. But the gunboats opened a galling fire that resulted in routing the enemy,

and in the death of General Green. Later, on
Porter's representation, Banks was relieved by
General Canby, and although in some quarters
attempts were made to shift part of the blame on

THE BOMBARDMENT OF FORT FISHER.

(From a wartime woodcut.)

Porter, public opinion awarded him the full
measure of praise for his share in the unfortunate
undertaking.

In September, 1864, he was placed in command of the North Atlantic Squadron, and
ordered to co-operate with General Butler in the
reduction of Fort Fisher and the other defenses

of Wilmington, N. C. On the night of December 24, 1864, he began a bombardment of the fort with a fleet of thirty-five vessels, five of which were iron- **ATTACK ON FORT FISHER** clads, and in about an hour its guns were silenced. General Butler, however, concluding that the works were not materially injured, and could not be carried by assault, returned to Hampton Roads. But Porter, who was of a different opinion, insisted on renewing the attack, and wrote to General Grant, requesting that the same troops be sent back under another general. He asserted that in this way the place could be taken, and his judg- **FALL OF FORT FISHER** ment proved correct. On January 15, 1865, with forty-four vessels in a curved line, and fourteen more held in reserve, he opened a terrible bombardment of the fort, driving the enemy into their bomb-proofs, silencing their guns and dismounting so many of them that by the time the co-operating land force under General Terry was ready for the assault the fort was so weak that it surrendered after a few hours' fighting. For this service Porter again received the thanks of Congress,

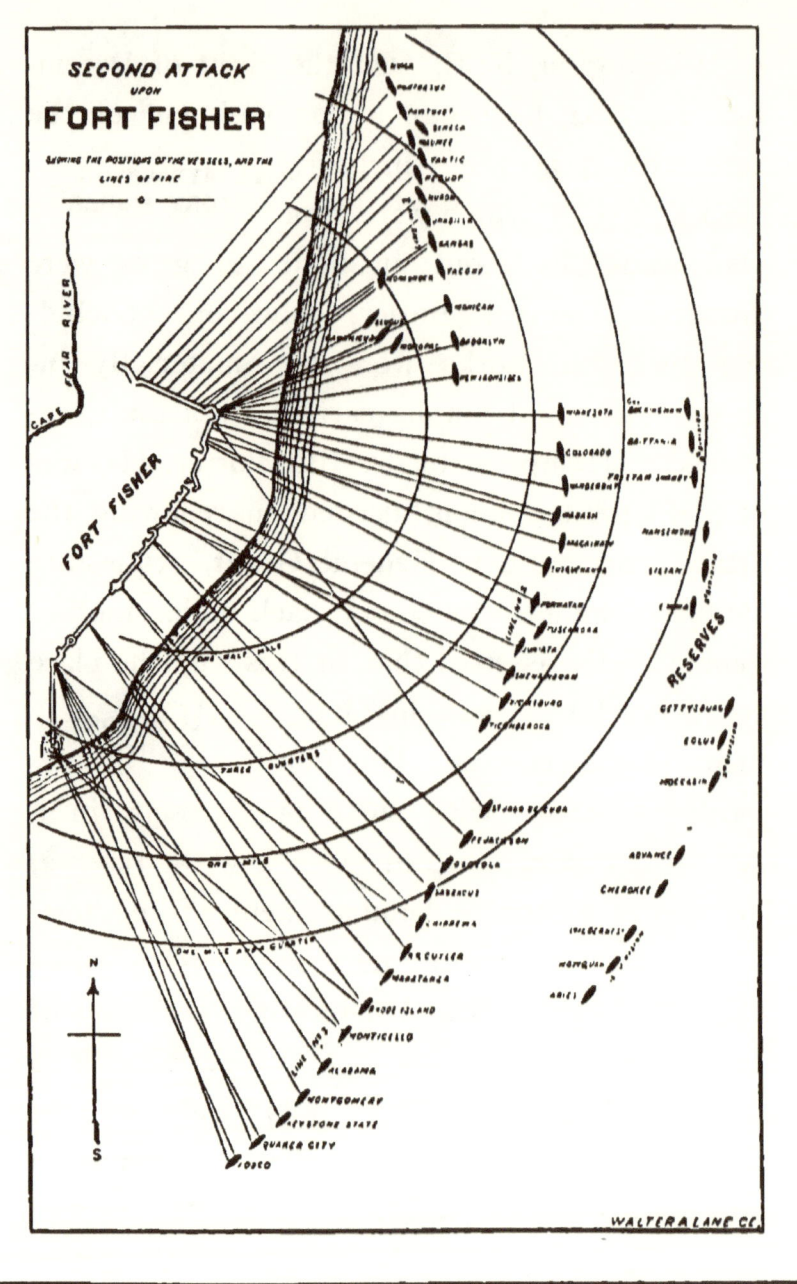

as well as of most of the State Legislatures of the Union.

The fall of Fort Fisher and Wilmington, N. C., virtually ended the war, closing the last of the Southern ports to the importation of supplies from abroad. Porter's last duty in the Civil War was in forcing IN THE JAMES his way up the James River as far RIVER as City Point, Prince George County, Va., where with a fleet of gunboats he participated in the final operations against Richmond. The night before the evacuation, April 2, 1865, he opened fire at long range on the enemy's works along the river, and the noise of the cannonade being interpreted by Rear-Admiral Raphael Semmes to indicate the advance of the Federal fleet, caused him to order the destruction of all the vessels under his command. Two days later, Porter accompanied President Lincoln into Richmond in triumph, having penetrated the length of the river with his smaller gunboats. Admiral Porter thus practically opened and ended the naval part of the Civil War ; having fired the first gun at Pensacola, April 17, 1861, and almost the last, in the vicinity of Richmond in 1865.

On September 9, 1865, he was appointed Superintendent of the United States Naval Academy, Annapolis, Md., continuing in that office until December 1, 1869. Here his great executive ability and wide experience in the needs of practical naval equipment were of the greatest service in the upbuilding and enlargement of the institution. Meantime, in 1866, he was commissioned by President Johnson to arrange a lease of Samana Bay, San Domingo, and the adjacent territory, on the basis of a bonus of $200,000.

SUPERIN-TENDENT AT ANNAPOLIS

He was, however, unable to conclude the negotiations on account of the obstinacy of the Dominican Government, and the project accordingly was abandoned. After his resignation from the Superintendency of the Naval Academy, in 1869, he was continuously retained on special duty in the Navy Department until 1890.

A DIPLO-MATIC SERVICE

When the grades of general and lieutenant-general were awarded to Grant and Sherman after the Civil War, those of admiral and vice-admiral were bestowed on Farragut and Porter, and on Farra-

PROMOTIONS

gut's death in 1870 Porter succeeded him as admiral, it being provided that the title should lapse at his death. He received three votes of thanks from Congress for services at Arkansas Post, Vicksburg, and Fort Fisher respectively— a distinction never accorded to any other naval commander.

Admiral Porter employed his leisure time in his later years largely in literary composition. He produced his "Life of Commodore David Porter" in 1875, and his "History of the Navy in the War of the Rebellion" in 1887. The latter work is still regarded as an authority on LITERARY EFFORTS the subject, and has been widely quoted. His other books are "Allan Dare and Robert le Diable" (1885); "Incidents and Anecdotes of the Civil War" (1885); "Harry Martine" (1886), and numerous essays and reports of great value and interest. He took a pardonable pride in the success of his novels, and as an indication of their merit, it may be mentioned that his "Allan Dare" was dramatized and successfully presented on the stage.

Admiral Porter was married March 11, 1839,

to Georgia Ann, daughter of Commodore Daniel

**MARRIAGE
AND FAMILY**
Tod Patterson, who commanded the naval forces co-operating with General Jackson at the battle of New Orleans, a service for which he received the thanks of Congress by name.   She was a sister of Captain Carlile P. Patterson, Superintendent of the United States Coast Survey (1874–81), and of Rear-Admiral Thomas H. Patterson, United States Navy.   They had four sons: Major Essex Porter, United States Army, retired; Lieutenant-Colonel Carlile P. Porter, of the United States Marine Corps ; Lieutenant-Commander Theodoric Porter, United States Navy, and Richard B. Porter, Chief Yeoman, United States Navy; and two daughters, the elder, wife of Captain Leavitt C. Logan, United States Navy, and the younger, wife of Charles H. Campbell.

Admiral Porter died at his home in Washing-

DEATH
ton, D. C., February 13, 1891. On that occasion the Secretary of the Navy issued the following general order :

NAVY DEPARTMENT, ⎱
February 13, 1891. ⎰

The Secretary of the Navy has the painful duty

of announcing to the Navy and the country
the death of the highest officer of the service. David Dixon Porter, Admiral of the
Navy, died at Washington, at 8.15 o'clock
this morning, in the seventy-eighth year of
his age. Sixty years of Admiral Porter's

A NOBLE life were actively devoted to the
TRIBUTE service of his country. The
record of his deeds forms one of the brightest
pages of its history. His achievements while
in command of the mortar flotilla of the Mississippi Squadron at the attack on the New
Orleans forts and at the fall of Vicksburg, and of
the North Atlantic Squadron at the capture of
Fort Fisher, have given him a place among the
foremost of the world's naval commanders. He
dies lamented by the whole country, and his
memory will forever be cherished and held in
honor by the service. On the day of the funeral
the Navy Department will be closed, the flag will
be displayed at half mast at all the navy yards
and stations and on board all ships in commission,
and seventeen minute guns will be fired at noon
from each navy yard. The Navy Department
will be draped, and all officers of the Navy and

Marine Corps will wear the badge of mourning for thirty days.

    (Signed)   B. F. TRACY.

   The Admiral and his wife are buried at Arlington, in front of the old Custis home on the hill overlooking the City of Washington. A heroic statue has been planned for Franklin Square in that city, and another to stand south of the City Hall in Philadelphia, Pa.

THE UNITED STATES IRONCLAD FRIGATE "NEW IRONSIDES"
OF THE ATLANTIC SQUADRON.

(*From a wartime woodcut.*)

GEORGE DEWEY

DEWEY

GEORGE DEWEY, the third Admiral of the United States BIRTH AND PARENTAGE Navy, was born in
Montpelier, Washington County, Vt., December 26, 1837, son of Julius Yemans and Mary (Perrin) Dewey.

His father (1801–77) was a practicing physician in Montpelier; his mother (1799–1843) was a daughter of Zachariah Perrin, of Gilead, Conn. He is eighth in descent from Thomas Dewey, of Sandwich, Kent, England, who, about 1633, emigrated to Massachusetts, and **ANCESTRY** in 1634 was admitted a freeman at Dorchester. This Thomas removed to Windsor, Conn., probably with Reverend Mr. Wareham's company, in 1636; was a juror in 1642–44, and died, April 27, 1648. Mrs. Frances Clark, to whom he was married in 1639, bore him a daughter and four sons, the second of whom,

Josiah, was the ancestor of the Admiral ; she was married for the third time to George Phelps, of Windsor, and later, with all her children but one, removed to Westfield, Mass. Josiah Dewey was married, in 1662, to Hepzibah, daughter of Richard Lyman, of Northampton, Mass., whose lineage, some genealogists claim, has been traced back through the Lambert family to Alfred the Great. He removed from Westfield to Lebanon, Conn., and in that town were born his son, Josiah, his great-grandson, Simeon, and probably his great-great-grandson, William (1746–1813). William, second of the name, became an early settler of Hanover, N. H. His son, Captain Simeon Dewey (1770–1863), grandfather of the Admiral, removed to Berlin, Vt., and subsequently to Montpelier, where he cultivated a farm.

George Dewey was the ringleader of the boys at Montpelier in their sports as well as in many

BOYHOOD a mischievous prank. He attended school in Montpelier and at Johnson, Vt., and in 1853 was admitted to Norwich University, Norwich, Vt. By that time he had decided to enter the United States

Naval Academy, and through the influence of
United States Senator Solomon Foot was appointed in 1854. He was grad-   NAVAL
uated with honor in 1858 in a   ACADEMY
class conspicuous for the number of its members
distinguished in after years.

In 1858–59 he was attached to the steam
frigate " Wabash " of the Mediterranean
Squadron; his year's work at that station giving
him the necessary experience for much of the responsibility later to be placed in his charge. He
was commissioned lieutenant,   EARLY
April 19, 1861, and assigned to   SERVICE
the steam sloop " Mississippi," of the West
Gulf Squadron, seeing his first service under
fire in the fleet with which Farragut reduced the
defences of the Mississippi River, below New
Orleans, in 1862.

In this immortal fight the " Mississippi," with
Dewey as executive officer, bore herself with distinguished credit, although the oldest vessel of
the squadron and the only side-wheeler. On the
appearance of the dreaded ram " Manassas " the
destruction of one or more of the Federal ships
seemed imminent, but the " Mississippi " pushed

forward to close with the iron terror. Apparently avoiding her, the "Manassas" ran off for a considerable distance, and then coming about, made for her under full head of steam. Dewey, who was at that time on the bridge, seemingly

ENCOUNTER OF THE "MISSISSIPPI" AND MANASSAS."

unmoved by the grave danger at hand, was quietly giving an order to a sub-

BATTLE IN THE MISSISSIPPI

ordinate officer. On a sudden the "Mississippi," swerving to one side and then hauling up sharp, opened her broadside on the enemy, piercing her armor in a

dozen places, setting her on fire, and sending her
floating down stream to explode opposite the
forts.

At the attempted passage of the Port Hudson
batteries, when the "Hartford"
alone of all the American ships
succeeded in keeping on her
course, the "Mississippi" persisted until riddled
with shot and shell. Being then run ashore and
set on fire, the crew escaped in boats; Lieutenant
Dewey being the last to step from the deck.

LOSS OF THE "MISSIS-SIPPI"

In his report of the disaster Captain Smith
says: "I consider that I should be neglecting a
most important duty should I omit to mention
the coolness of my executive officer, Mr. Dewey,
and the steady, fearless and gallant manner in
which the officers and men of the 'Mississippi'
defended her, and the orderly and quiet manner
in which she was abandoned after being thirty-
five minutes aground under the fire of the
enemy's batteries."

Among his last engagements in the Mississippi
were the attacks on the batteries at Donaldson-
ville, La. During 1864–65 he was attached to the
steam gunboat "Agawam," of the North Atlantic

Blockading Squadron, participating in the attacks on Fort Fisher in December, 1864, and January, 1865. On March 3, 1865, he was commissioned lieutenant-commander for meritorious conduct in both attacks on Fort Fisher. He was ordered to the "Kearsarge" in 1866, and to the "Colo-

UNITED STATES STEAM SLOOP "MISSISSIPPI."

rado" in 1867, flagship of the European Squad-

AFTER THE WAR ron. He returned home in 1868, and for two years thereafter was instructor in the Naval Academy. In 1870–71 he was in command of the fourth-rater "Narragansett" on special service; was commissioned commander, April 13, 1872, and then for three years was with the Pacific survey. He served as

Lighthouse Inspector in 1876–77, then became Secretary of the Lighthouse Board, and in 1882–83, commanded the "Juni- AMONG THE
ata" on the Asiatic Station. LIGHTHOUSES

He was promoted captain in 1884, and was placed in command of the "Dolphin," one of the original "White Squadron." In 1885 he returned to the European Station in command of the "Pensacola," the flagship of the squadron, remaining there until 1888, when he was ordered home, and appointed Chief of the Bureau of Equipment and Recruiting with the title of commodore. In May, 1893, he was appointed a member of the Lighthouse Board. On February 26, 1896, he was commissioned commodore, and made President of the Board of Inspec- THE ASIATIC
tion and Survey, which position STATION
he held until the fall of 1897, when he was appointed to the command of the Asiatic Station.

While at Hong Kong, in March, 1898, Prince Henry, of Germany, arrived at that port with his squadron, and gave a banquet to the higher officers of the fleets lying in the harbor. During the meal the Prince proposed toasts to the various peoples represented, including China, but omitted the United States, whereupon Commodore Dewey left the table without ceremony.

A SLIGHT RESENTED He refused to accept anything but a written personal apology from the Prince, who later made a personal call to explain that the neglect to mention the United States was unintentional. Later Prince Henry gave a ball, but Commodore Dewey, although invited, did not attend.

Ten days after the destruction of the " Maine " in Havana Harbor, Commodore Dewey received orders from the Navy Department to concentrate his squadron, and be in readiness to attack the Spanish naval forces in the Philippines in case war should prove the outcome of the existing complications. The vessels of the Asiatic Squadron forthwith assembled at Hong Kong from their several stations: the " Boston " and " Concord " from Korea; the " Raleigh " and " McCulloch " from Indian waters, and the " Baltimore " from Honolulu. The two small steamers " Nan-Shan " and " Zafiro " were purchased for colliers or tenders.

MOBILIZING THE SQUADRON

The War with Spain opened April 21, 1898, and three days later President McKinley, through the Secretary of the Navy, cabled the following orders to **PREPARE FOR WAR** Dewey at Hong Kong: "Proceed at once to the Philippine Islands. Commence operations, particularly against the Spanish fleet. You must capture or destroy the vessels. Use utmost endeavor."

In pursuance of this order, the Asiatic Squadron, comprising the "Olympia" (flagship), "Baltimore," "Boston," "Raleigh," "Concord," and "Petrel," with the revenue cutter "McCulloch," as auxiliary despatch boat, sailed on April 27th from Mirs Bay. They made the passage of the China Sea at leisurely speed, and reached Cape Bolinao on the morning of the 30th.

Firmly expecting to find the Spanish fleet mobilized in Subig Bay, according to the advice of some of **A STILL HUNT** the best Spanish strategists—strangely enough one of them had in 1891 written a pamphlet anticipating the very course of action adopted by Dewey, and warning his countrymen

accordingly—the " Boston " and the " Concord "
were sent forward to reconnoitre, supported by
the " Baltimore." The course was then steered
to Manila Bay. Under the cover of the night
THE BAY OF   the squadron crept through the
MANILA   wider channel, the Boca Grande,
past the batteries of Corregidor Island, and
into the open water beyond. All lights were
extinguished, and but for a spark emitted
from the " McCulloch's " funnel the passage
would have been entirely unobserved. That
was a signal to the Spaniards, who, forthwith,
opened fire, and were promptly answered by the
" Raleigh," " Boston " and " Concord."

The passage was remarkable not only in its
effect, but also for the display of intrepid bravery
in going forward despite mines and torpedoes
and the galling fire of batteries reported impregnable, and Commodore Dewey's feat is, for
AN ECHO OF   dash and gallantry, worthy to
FARRAGUT   rank with Farragut's memorable
defiance of the forts below New Orleans. It
is a conspicuous instance of a grand example
grandly followed. In planning the move, mines,
batteries and other defenses were simply

ignored ; there was neither dragging, dodging, nor change from the direct course. Contrary to expectation the Spanish fleet did not appear to give fight to the invading Americans under support of the shore batteries, and Dewey, accordingly, held his course direct for the city.

The Battle of Manila Bay began at 5.15 on the morning of May 1, 1898, when the shore batteries of Manila and Cavité and the Spanish fleet, sheltered behind Sangley **IN LINE OF** Point, opened fire on the Amer- **BATTLE** ican ships. The Spaniards, thus sheltered, awaited Dewey's approaching line, headed by the flagship " Olympia," with the " Baltimore," " Raleigh," " Petrel," " Concord," and " Boston" following in succession. The American firing did not begin until 5.41 A.M., when, having sufficiently observed the wild cannonade and evident intentions of the enemy, Commodore Dewey gave his memorable direction: " You may fire when you are ready, Gridley." Two mines were exploded ahead of the " Olympia," too far away to be effective, and she and her companions bore steadily forward, countermarching in a line approximately parallel to that of the

Spanish fleet, and maintaining a constant cannonade, wonderful for its precision, at ranges varying
COMPLETE from 5,000 to 2,000 yards. It
DESTRUCTION took just five turns to do the
work. The effect of the American fire was terrific in its destructiveness, and the Spanish ships,
being disabled one after another, were run
aground, sunk or blown up. One of them,
the "Don Antonio de Ulloa" attempted to keep
up the fight, but was soon sunk by the American
fire. At 7.35 A.M. Dewey withdrew his squadron for breakfast to the middle of the bay, and
returning to the attack at 11.16, completed the
work of destruction in a little less than two
hours; the whole Spanish fleet of twelve vessels
being left hopeless wrecks.

In the early part of the fight the land batteries
of Manila maintained an incessant fire, to which
the American squadron made no reply, but Commodore Dewey effectively silenced them by a message threatening to shell the city if they continued. Although holding no high opinion of
Spanish marksmanship, he provided to protect
his own ships by a continual forward movement
that prevented the gunners from finding the

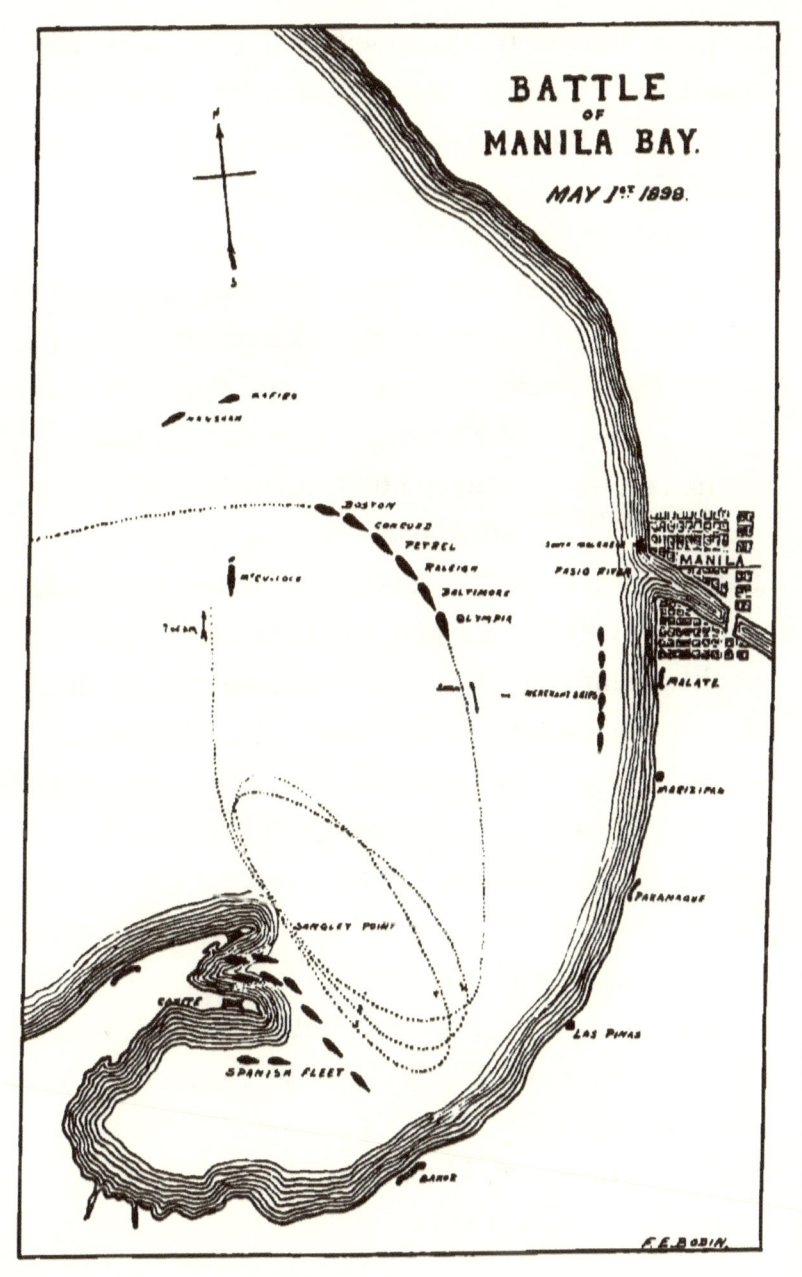

range in time to do them serious harm, with the
result that but few shells struck the American
ships.   In the course of the action the "Don
Juan de Austria," and later also the "Reina
Cristina" made a dash at the "Olympia," with
evident intention of ramming or using torpedoes,
but the steady fire of the American gunners
drove both back in flames to run aground near

the shore.   Two small launches,
**A
RESISTLESS
CANNONADE** believed to be torpedo-boats, were
discovered in the path of the
flagship, one being sunk, the other wrecked.
As was afterward alleged, the latter was a private
yacht, bent on domestic business in Manila.
A few well-aimed shots from the "Raleigh"
brought down the Spanish flag at Cavité after
the naval force had been utterly vanquished, and
crews in whale-boats pulled ashore to complete
the work of destruction and capture any launches
or tugboats found afloat.

The American loss was seven wounded, the
Spanish, over 200 killed.   All the Spanish vessels
were destroyed—"Reina Cristina," "Castilla,"
"Don Antonio de Ulloa," sunk; "Don Juan de
Austria," "Isla de Luzon," "Isla de Cuba,"

"General Lezo," "Marques del Duero," "Argos," "Velasco," and "Isle de Mindanao," burned. On May 4th Commodore Dewey sent the following dispatch:

"I have taken possession of the naval station at Cavité. Have destroyed the fortifications at bay entrance, paroling garrison. I control bay completely and can take city at any time. The squadron is in ex- *VENI, VIDI, VICI* cellent health and spirits. Spanish loss not fully known, but very heavy. One hundred and fifty killed, including the captain of the ' Reina Cristina.' I am assisting in protecting the Spanish sick and wounded. Two hundred and fifty sick and wounded in hospital within our lines. Much excitement at Manila. Will protect foreign residents."

Contrary to the expectation of the Spaniards, Manila was not bombarded, and on this account the Governor-General defied the American authority for several weeks, although a strict blockade of the port was maintained.

The complete annihilation of the Spanish fleet at Manila aroused enthusiasm throughout the civilized world, and Commodore Dewey was at once appointed acting rear-admiral by President McKinley, and shortly after confirmed by

THE THANKS OF A NATION Congress in the appointment to the full rank. On May 9th the President sent a special message to Congress which contained this splendid tribute:

" The magnitude of this victory can hardly be measured by the ordinary standards of naval warfare. Outweighing any material advantage is the moral effect of this initial success. At this unsurpassed achievement the great heart of our nation throbs, not with boasting or with greed of conquest, but with deep gratitude that this triumph has come in a just cause, and that by the grace of God an effective step has thus been taken toward the attainment of the wished-for peace." The message concluded : " I now recommend that, following our national precedents, and expressing the fervent gratitude of every patriotic heart, the thanks of Congress be given Rear-Admiral George Dewey, of the United States Navy, for highly distinguished conduct in conflict with the enemy, and to the officers and men under his command for their gallantry in the destruction of the enemy's fleet and the capture of the enemy's fortifications in the Bay of Manila.''

The surrender of Manila was preceded by seri-

UNITED STATES UNARMORED CRUISER "OLYMPIA."

ous fighting all along the American lines, and after the capitulation the situation became enormously com- **THE AFTERMATH OF THE WAR** plicated, requiring the greatest coolness and the most positive determination, until the arrival of reinforcements in sufficient number and a military governor relieved him of the responsibility. Not only were the trying and annoying acts on the part of the Filipinos under their cunning and aggressive chief, Aguinaldo, most difficult to meet, but disturbing incidents in connection with the acts of the German Admiral at Manila, frequently threatened to precipitate international complications.

Through all these perplexities, Dewey displayed the calm positiveness of a master and the diplomatic genius of an experienced statesman. His achievements in arms and after, through THE REWARD OF HEROISM all the trying scenes of the Philippine revolt against the establishment of American power in the islands, determined President McKinley to yield to the popular demand and recommend the revival, in favor of Dewey, of the rank of admiral, previously held only by Farragut and David D. Porter, and vacant since the latter's death in 1891. Accordingly, on March 3, 1899, the appointment was confirmed in executive session of the United States Senate, making Dewey not only ranking officer in the Navy, but the superior of all others in either service, since major-generals are rated on a parity with rear-admirals.

Having been finally relieved of command at Manila on his own request, Admiral Dewey set sail on his return voyage to the United States in the cruiser " Olympia," May 20, 1899, and after a leisurely journey, *via* the Suez Canal, touching at most of the important points, he arrived at home in the early autumn.

It is, perhaps, unexampled in history that an officer should serve his government faithfully, courageously, and often under the most dangerous conditions, should pass without special public note through the different grades of rank to near the highest, and then at the age of sixty, by one marvellous feat of inspired daring, overshadow all the great records of the world. Nelson was great before Trafalgar; Napoleon superb before Austerlitz and Marengo; Grant magnificent before Appomattox; but to Dewey there seemed to come at Manila, once and for all time, the audacity, as well as the inspiration, which raised him, as by one stroke, to the immortal peerage of naval heroism.

THE INSPIRATION OF GENIUS

Vice-Admiral Philip Howard Colomb, a retired English naval officer of great distinction, wrote shortly after the battle: "I doubt if there ever was such an extraordinary illustration of the influence of sea power. An American fleet has attacked and beaten a Spanish fleet supported

by batteries, and it now appears it passed these
batteries and has taken up an unassailable posi-
ENGLAND TO tion off Manila. The boldness
AMERICA of the American commander is
beyond question. Henceforth he must be
placed in the Valhalla of great naval commanders.
Nothing can detract from the dash and vigor of
the American exploit, or dim the glory which
Dewey has shed upon the American Navy. It
may be bad for the world, for assuredly the
American Navy will never accept a subordinate
place after this exhibition of what it can do.''

John D. Long, Secretary of the Navy, wrote
some months after the war : '' This victory (at
Manila Bay) made Commodore Dewey deservedly
famous, and gave him rank among the most distinguished naval heroes of all time. Nor was his
merit most in the brilliant victory which he
THE GLORY achieved. . . . It was still
OF OUR NAVY more in the nerve with which
he moved from Mirs Bay to Manila harbor;
. . the high commanding confidence of
a leader who has weighed every risk, prepared himself for every emergency. . . .
It was a man of resolution and power, who, at

that vast distance from home, with his little fleet shut off by the neutrality laws from every port, and bearing the fate of his country in his hand, was equal to the emergency, and met it as serenely and masterfully as if it were an incident of an ordinary voyage."

Admiral Dewey was married at Portsmouth, N. H., October 24, 1867, to Susan B., daughter of ex-Governor Ichabod Good- **DEWEY'S** win, of Portsmouth, N. H. **MARRIAGE** She died in December, 1872, leaving a son, George Goodwin, who, after his graduation at Princeton College, entered business in New York City.

ADMIRAL'S FLAG OF THE UNITED STATES NAVY.